I0743081

Strong Memories

Alix Kelinda

Strong Memories

Radical Bookshop and Press
4838 Richard Road SW, Suite 300
Calgary, AB T3E 6L1

FIC029000 - Fiction, Short Stories

Chinook Blast Collection
Volume 1
February 1, 2021

Editors: Lexie Angelo
Cover Design: Lexie Angelo

ISBN-13: 978-1-990201-04-2

Printed in the United States

Typeset in Gibson

To Mom, of course.

contents

Strong Memories

I smile for the first time in weeks as I approach the archway. The letter L on the sign is slanted further right than I remember, even though this image has persisted in my mind like a photograph. I push through the turnstile. No payment is required. There is no bored teenaged attendant to slowly count my change while hoards of children shriek excitedly behind me. Today, this amusement park is mine alone.

For now, that is—until I change all that. I pat my pocket and check that the folded instructions are still there.

I pass the unoccupied bumper boats, the stationary carousel, the motionless mini express. There's a haunted feeling about the place. Every colour has been dipped in grey, as if a layer of dust covers the whole park, except when I go to wipe a surface my finger comes away clean. There isn't even the rustling of leaves or buzzing of insects to replace the missing sound of children's laughter. The park is dim and quiet.

A pale and hazy sun is frozen overhead. I wipe my brow out of habit but again my hand comes away clean.

The last time I was here beads of sweat slithered down from my hairline and pooled atop my collarbone, even though it was a cloudier day than this one. The July heat took a polite break that morning or I may not have made the trip at all. My family dropped me off right at the front gate to minimize my exertion, but just standing there, waiting for Jeremy to park the car, required effort. We didn't stay long, carefully selecting a handful of our favourite rides. Still, every step I took was like dragging forward an iron ball. Trying to conceal that fact from my daughters was even more exacting.

Now, however, I feel buoyant.

I jog and pick up speed. My stride turns into a half-skip but not quite a sprint. The eerie feel of this empty park disappears as I marvel at the absence of pain in my body. I dart up the stairs to the rollercoaster loading platform and zigzag through the empty queue. Oh, screw it. I hop the rail, cutting the invisible line, giddy as a schoolgirl.

I jump into one of the cars. The train doesn't move, but I lean sideways, shift forwards, and holler out with my hands raised high, letting my imagination take me on the ride. I picture my sweet girls, Chelsea and Samantha, waving at me from the ground as the coaster makes its long ascent before zooming downward at high speed. I love this ride, but I couldn't enjoy it last time because cancer's grip was too tight.

When the fantasy ride comes to an end, I sit contemplatively, reminding myself why I'm really here.

Returning to ground level, I pull out my instructions and unfold the paper.

I'm only reading the first line when I hear pebbles skitter behind me. The sudden intrusion of sound highlights the unnerving quiet of the park. I whip around. I don't see anything except a long lane of empty shops and vacant rides. The park reminds me of those old west ghost towns where a tumbleweed might tumble by. There's too much stillness here.

I return my attention to the sheet of paper in my hands.

Step 1. Select the spot associated with the strongest memories.

That's easy. I make my way to the cotton candy stand outside the spinning strawberries.

I remember the girls' squeals of delight as we went around and around and around some more, until Jeremy and I could take no more. With our stomachs reeling, we'd offer the girls a sweet treat in exchange for getting off the ride for the final time. It was a bribe that turned into a game, that turned into a tradition, with the girls spinning us faster and faster, and Jeremy flailing around the carriage like he was caught in a tornado, until we surrendered to their wishes.

Step 2. Write the desired date on the ground beneath your feet.

I pause to consider. Two years seems adequate. Next summer might be too soon, while anything after two years would feel too late, like happiness would never return if it hadn't by then.

My cancer-free bones don't even crackle as I kneel onto the pavement and scribble the year in white chalk followed by: *July 1.*

Footsteps.

I jump upright, looking behind me again. I feel certain I heard the patter of quick feet. I scan my surroundings more thoroughly this time, inspecting the strawberry ride, scrutinizing the food carts that line the footpath, searching for any sign of life. Or is that a misnomer in this abandoned place?

There.

A girl. With one long braid draped over her shoulder. She is spying out from behind the soft pretzel stand.

She reminds me of my Sam, with her watchful, curious demeanour. I smile, squat, and reach out a hand the way you might offer a treat to a skittish pet.

"Hello there," I say. "My name's Laura. What's yours?"

She hides behind the food stand, still young enough to believe that if she can't see me, I won't know she's there. Of course, who else would linger here except a child of her age? My smile falters. She's much too young and all alone.

 "Lovely park, isn't it?" I say. "My husband and my girls used to come here every year on Canada Day. My daughter, Samantha, especially liked the cotton candy. Chelsea too, although the pretzels were a close second. How about you?"

She doesn't reply but peeks out from her hiding spot.

"What's your favourite ride?" I ask. "Do you have one?"

She shakes her head, digging her toe into the pavement as if squishing an imaginary bug.

"No? Not even the flying eggshells?"

She frowns. "Before, maybe."

"But not now?

"Too quiet."

I know how she feels. "It is too quiet."

I peer down at my instructions.

"Do you want to help me? I'm going to bring back all the people and make the park lively again."

Her eyes spark to life and she steps out from behind the pretzel stand. "You are?"

"Yes," I say. "For a little while, anyway. I could sure use some help."

She trots toward me, stopping every two or three steps to re-evaluate her decision, eying me keenly.

"Okay," I say when she's finally at my side. "First things first, if you're going to be my helper, I need to know your name."

"Audrey," she declares, as if it's a source of pride.

"Audrey, what a pretty name."

She grins.

"Okay, Audrey. Here's what we're going to do. You need to listen very carefully."

I go over the directions with her step by step. We rehearse the chant, syllable by syllable. Maybe she has instructions of her own and this could be valuable practice.

"Now," I say once we're finished. "Are you ready for the real thing?"

She nods, bobbing eagerly on the pads of her feet.

We join hands. My index and thumb make a full circum-ference around her tiny palm. We start to turn, gathering momentum, until we're twirling in circles like we're a spinning strawberry. Audrey has a lovely voice, which grows stronger with each repetition, and soon we are singing, not chanting, bringing the sound of joy back into this haunted place. I arch my neck, looking to the sky. The sun swirls above me, yellowing, brightening. We sing louder, spurred on by the colours illuminating all around us. The strawberries grow red again rather than a pale pink. Then the noises arrive. Laughter, shrieks, chatter. "Mommy!" I hear someone shout, not to me, but I close my eyes and feel it as if it were Chelsea herself.

When I open my eyes again, Audrey and I are surrounded by a different scene. I see children dash by, their parents corralling, shouting, speed-walking to keep pace. Audrey gapes at me with round blue eyes and rushes over to join a group of children who are playing in the grass.

I watch her jump up and down and giggle alongside them, skipping when they skip, picking dandelions as they do. When she stumbles into one of the boys she passes right through him. She laughs and runs through him again.

"Look!" she shouts at me, waving her hands. "Look what I can do!"

She tosses her immaterial little frame through the boy, again and again, like it's a fantastic trick.

She doesn't understand.

I try not to let the sad truth show on my face, and I watch her for longer than I should, distracted from my purpose.

The new world flickers. The people briefly disappear then reappear. My heart somersaults. I'm wasting precious time.

I begin my search, scanning the ride and the long line for cotton candy. They aren't here. I jog down the pathway, darting around the masses to the children's bumper cars, Chelsea and Samantha's second-favourite ride. They aren't there either.

I tick off their favourite places one by one, growing more frantic with each elapsing minute. Another flicker. The crowd vanishes for two full seconds. I start running straight through people just like Audrey was doing. My chest is tight. Time is running out. Where could they be?

Maybe they didn't come.

No.

They must be here. They must be. What other ride might they—?

I skid to a complete stop. My breathing hitches. I turn around and sprint away from the kids rides, back the way I came.

I rush up the stairs to the rollercoaster loading platform and weave my way through the packed queue.

There!

Jeremy and the girls are loading into one of the carts. Chelsea hops right in, but Samantha hesitates.

Jeremy places his hands on her shoulders. "Are you sure you're not too scared?"

She shakes her head and puffs out her chest in a comical imitation of bravado. She's so much bigger now, that much taller.

"This was mommy's favourite ride," she says, determined. "So, it's mine too."

Jeremy tousles her hair and chuckles, just a hint of sadness leaking out from an otherwise happy moment. "Alright," he says. "Let's get you buckled in then."

The girls sit together, holding hands, with Jeremy right behind them. The cars click into motion and I watch their anxious faces as the train winds along the track. They pass by, unable to see me, and soon I can't see them anymore either. But I'm almost certain I can pick out each one of their voices—Jeremy, husky and theatrical, Samantha and Chelsea, high-pitched and genuinely thrilled—as the coaster speeds up and swings upside down.

Everyone blinks away for long seconds. I don't mind this time.

They're here. They're happy. That's all I needed to know.

Relief rolls through me, winding itself through my soul, much like the train on its track. Then I am floating, lifted upward by soft hands unseen.

I soar into the sky, gazing wistfully down at the fair in action, the way it's meant to be. Then I spot her. She's the only person looking up at me, growing smaller with each passing second. Our eyes interlock. And even though we're hundreds of meters apart, I know she can hear me because we're connected in a way that transcends corporeal limitations.

"Audrey," I yell. "Come with me!"

She shakes her head.

"Please," I shout. "Come."

I extend my hand to her. My limb appears blurred, my physical body already fading away.

Audrey stands, unmoving.

I rise higher and higher until she's nothing but a lone speck in a deserted park. There must be more for her to do. She's not ready yet.

But I am.

I close my eyes for the last time.

ACKNOWLEDGEMENTS

First, I'd like to thank the Alexandra Writers' Centre Society for providing the writing prompt that inspired this story. Thanks to my mom for reading everything I've ever written (more than once) and for taking me on the spinning strawberries a hundred times. Thanks to all my wonderful and supportive friends. Lastly, to my husband, for listening patiently while I think out loud whenever a new idea sparks.

ABOUT THE AUTHOR

Alix has an undergraduate degree in Psychology, a masters degree in Medical Sciences, and a certificate in Creative Writing. She won second place in the 2019 Robyn Herrington Short Story Contest (published in In Places Between) and has another short story published in Treasures Along the Fenceline. Her current novel-length projects include two contemporaries with strong romantic undertones and an upmarket apocalyptic love story. She enjoys helping her characters find love and humour amidst grief and tragedy. Regardless of genre, her writing is introspective, delving deep into the psychological layers that make human beings flawed and interesting. When not writing, she works as a biostatistician analyzing healthcare data. She can also be found climbing rocks, reading books, and drinking wine.

Visit her website www.alixkelinda.com.

Follow on Twitter: @KelindaAlix.

Follow on Instagram: @KelindaAlixWrites

SPECIAL THANKS

Chinook Blast Festival

The City of Calgary

Tourism Calgary

Calgary Municipal Land Corporation

Calgary Arts Development

Calgary Public Library

IngramSpark